2/14/14

TO: Orly
Love: Mom &
        Dad

I Like You

by Sandol Stoddard Warburg

illustrated by Jacqueline Chwast

Houghton Mifflin Books for Children
Houghton Mifflin Harcourt
Boston

Houghton Mifflin Books for Children is an imprint of Houghton Mifflin
Harcourt Publishing Company.

www.hmhbooks.com

LIBRARY OF CONGRESS CATALOG CARD NUMBER 65-11020
ISBN-13: 978-0-395-07176-2
PRINTED IN CHINA

SCP 55 54 53 52
4500398681

to Jean
and Frank
and Marian
and Paul
and Matthew
and Joy
and Austin
and people
like that

I like you
And I know why

I like you because
You are a good person
To like

I like you because

When I tell you something special
You know it's special
And you remember it
A long long time

You say remember when
    you told me
Something special

And both of us remember

When I think something is important
You think it's important too

We have good ideas

When I say something funny

You laugh

I think I'm funny and
You think I'm funny too

Hah-hah

I like you because
You know where I'm ticklish
And you don't tickle me there
        except
        Just a little tiny bit
                sometimes

stop
    stop stop
    help
help

But if you do then I know where to tickle you too

HELP

You know how to be silly
That's why I like you
Boy are you ever silly

I never met anybody sillier than me

till I met you

I like you because
You know when it's time to stop being silly

Maybe day after tomorrow
Maybe never

Oops too late
It's quarter past silly

We fool around the same way all the time

Sometimes we don't say a word
We snurkle under fences
We spy secret places

If I am a goofus on the roofus
Hollering my head off
You are one too

If I pretend I am drowning
You pretend you are saving me

If I am getting ready to pop a paper bag
Then you are getting ready to jump

HOORAY

That's because
You really like me

You really like me
Don't you

And I really like you back
And you like me back
And I like you back

And that's the way we keep on going
Every day

If you go away then I go away too
Or if I stay home
You send me a postcard

You don't just say
Well see you around
Some time
Bye

I like you a lot because of that
If I go away
I send you a postcard too

And I like you because
If we go away together
And if we are in Grand Central Station
And if I get lost
Then you are the one that is yelling for me

Hey where are you

Here I am

And I like you because
When I am feeling sad
You don't always cheer me up right away

Sometimes it is better to be sad
You can't stand the others being so googly and gaggly
   every single minute
You want to think about things

It takes time

I like you because if I am mad at you
Then you are mad at me too

It's awful when the other person isn't

Phooey

They are so nice and hoo-hoo you could
just about punch them in the nose

I like you because if I think I am going to
throw up then you are really sorry

You don't just pretend you are busy looking at
the birdies and all that

You say maybe it was something you ate

You say the same thing happened to me one time

And the same thing did

If you find two four-leaf clovers
You give me one

If I find four
I give you two

If we only find three
We keep on looking

Sometimes we have good luck
And sometimes we don't

If I break my arm and
If you break your arm too
Then it is fun to have a broken arm

I tell you about mine
You tell me about yours

We are both sorry

We write our names and draw pictures

We show everybody and they wish they had
a broken arm too

I like you because
I don't know why but
Everything that happens
Is nicer with you

I can't remember when I didn't like you

It must have been lonesome then

I like you because because because

I forget why I like you

But I do

So many reasons

On the Fourth of July
I like you because
It's the Fourth of July

On the Fifth of July
I like you too

If you and I had some drums
And some horns and some horses

If we had some hats and some
Flags and some fire engines

We could be a HOLIDAY
We could be a CELEBRATION

We could be a WHOLE PARADE
See what I mean?

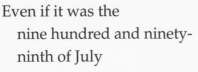

Even if it was the
  nine hundred and ninety-
  ninth of July

Even if it was
  August

Even if it was way down at the bottom of November
Even if it was no place particular in January

I would go on choosing you
And you would
    go on choosing me
Over and over again

That's how it would happen every time
I don't know why

I guess I don't know why I like you really
Why do I like you

I guess I just like you

I guess I just like you

Because I like you